ABOUT THIS BOOK

The Fourth Floor Twins and the Fish Snitch Mystery
DAVID A. ADLER
Illustrated by Irene Trivas

Where have the "nice" old couple hidden their nephew? And why are newspapers vanishing from their doorstep? Something fishy is going on, but the Fourth Floor Twins aren't fooled. Donna and Diane, Eric's identical twin sisters in the *Cam Jansen Adventure Series*, join their fourth floor neighbors, twins Gary and Kevin, in a suspenseful double mystery—sure to keep you reeling with laughter!

"Young readers and listeners will be delighted with this series."
—*School Library Journal*

The Fourth Floor Twins and the Fish Snitch Mystery

DAVID A. ADLER
Illustrated by Irene Trivas

Puffin Books

PUFFIN BOOKS
Viking Penguin Inc., 40 West 23rd Street, New York, New York 10010, U.S.A.
Penguin Books Ltd, Harmondsworth, Middlesex, England
Penguin Books Australia Ltd, Ringwood, Victoria, Australia
Penguin Books Canada Limited, 2801 John Street, Markham, Ontario, Canada L3R 1B4
Penguin Books (N.Z.) Ltd, 182–190 Wairau Road, Auckland 10, New Zealand

First published by Viking Penguin Inc. 19855Published in Puffin Books 1986

Printed in U.S.A.
by R. R. Donnelley & Sons Company, Harrisonburg, Virginia
Set in Times Roman

Library of Congress Cataloging in Publication Data
Adler, David A. The fourth floor twins and the fish snitch mystery.
Summary: Two sets of twins suspect their neighbors of wrongdoing when they observe the strange behavior of the couple's nephew.
[1. Twins—Fiction. 2. Mystery and detective stories] I. Trivas, Irene, ill. II. Title.
PZ7.A2615Fm 1986 [Fic] 85-43408 ISBN 0-14-032082-2

To my good friends
Elliot, Barbara, and Etan

The Fourth Floor Twins and the Fish Snitch Mystery

In this series

The Fourth Floor Twins and the Fish Snitch Mystery

The Fourth Floor Twins and the Fortune Cookie Chase

Also by David A. Adler

The Cam Jansen Adventure Series
Illustrated by Susanna Natti

CHAPTER ONE

"I wish I had enough money to buy a kangaroo," Gary Young said.

It was the first day of spring vacation. Gary and his twin brother Kevin were walking home from the park. Their friends Donna and Diane Shelton were with them.

"I wish I had enough money to buy a kangaroo," Gary said again.

"We heard you," Donna told him. "We're just not interested in another dumb joke."

"I'm going to be a comedian. I have to tell jokes."

"Last week you were going to be a plumber. Before that it was a lawyer and a bank teller," Donna said. "I can't keep up with you."

The children came to their apartment building. Max the doorman was outside digging. On the ground nearby were a few pieces of long, black hose.

"Good afternoon, my Fourth Floor Twins," Max said. "While you were playing in the park, I was working. I'm putting in an underground sprinkler system. I'll be able to water the grass without pulling the hoses out. They'll be buried."

Gary rubbed his chin, as if he was thinking about something important. Then he told Max, "I wish I had enough money to buy a kangaroo."

"What do you want with a kangaroo?" Max asked.

"I don't want the kangaroo. I just want the money!" Gary laughed at his own joke.

"Hm," Max said. "Will you hand me a piece of hose?"

Donna and Diane Shelton live on the fourth floor of the apartment building. They're identical twins. But they don't look exactly alike. Donna braids her hair. Diane's hair hangs straight down.

Gary and Kevin Young live on the fourth floor, too. They're twins, but they are not identical. Kevin is taller. He has straight hair and freckles. Gary has curly hair and he wears eyeglasses.

"Do you know what goes *zzub, zzub?* It's a bee going backward," Gary said. "And did you hear about the man who was playing a harmonica? He swallowed it. The doctor told him, 'You're lucky you weren't playing a piano.' "

Gary looked at Max. Then he looked at

Kevin, Donna, and Diane. No one had laughed. No one even smiled.

"Please give me another piece of hose," Max said.

"I read about a comedian with eyeglasses like yours," Kevin said. "His name was Harold Lloyd. But *he* was funny. In one movie, he was standing on the ledge of a tall building. A mouse crawled up his leg and he almost fell off the ledge."

Donna and Diane smiled. Gary didn't. He said, "That's a little funny. But swallowing a piano is funnier."

"Oh, look," Max said. "Here come the Wilsons from apartment 2B. That boy with them is their nephew Barry. This morning I helped them carry in his luggage. He's visiting for spring vacation."

The twins saw an old couple and a boy walk toward them. The man was holding the boy's hand. He seemed to be pulling the boy.

"Hi," Diane said.

The man pulled the boy past the children. "Don't talk to them," he told his nephew.

"And don't go near them," his aunt said, as she opened the door to the apartment building. The twins watched through the window as the Wilsons and their nephew went into the elevator.

"What's wrong with us?" Donna asked.

CHAPTER TWO

"Those two old people are strange," Kevin said.

"No, they're really very nice," Max said. "Mr. Wilson worked in a shoe store. He's retired now. And Mrs. Wilson works in the library."

The twins helped Max connect the hoses. Max attached the sprinkler heads.

"They never had children of their own," Max said, as he covered the hoses with dirt.

"They were all excited when Barry came. They plan to take him all over the city—to museums, the zoo, and the circus."

"We're going to the City Museum tomorrow," Diane said. "Maybe Barry wants to come with us."

Max covered all the hoses with dirt. He smoothed the dirt so it was even with the grass. Then he turned the sprinkler heads so the water would spray on the grass and not on the sidewalk.

"This green grass reminds me of a joke," Gary said. "Do you know what's big, fat, and green? It's a moldy elephant. And you know what's small, green, and dangerous? A frog with a gun."

"Those jokes aren't funny," Donna said.

Max picked up his shovel and tool box. "I'm done," he told the twins. "I'm going in to turn on the water. Stand on the sidewalk so you don't get wet."

"You should study what makes people

laugh," Kevin told Gary. "Harold Lloyd made a movie called *Speedy*. Then he went to the theater and saw which jokes got the biggest laughs."

"Gary can't do that," Donna said. "None of his jokes get laughs. I think he should become a bank teller."

Just then the sprinklers went on. Water sprayed onto the sidewalk and the twins. They ran to the grass where it was dry.

"Hey," Max said as he came out of the building. "What are you doing on the lawn? You'll get wet."

Max walked on the sidewalk toward the children. Water sprayed onto his face and clothes.

"I better shut this off," Max said. And he went back into the building.

The water stopped. Then, as the twins returned to the sidewalk, Gary asked, "Did you hear about the six fat women who were standing under one tiny umbrella? Do you

know why they didn't get wet? It wasn't raining."

As the twins walked into the building, the elevator door opened. Mrs. Wilson walked out.

"We're going to the City Museum to-morrow," Diane told her. "Maybe Barry wants to come with us."

Mrs. Wilson didn't answer. She walked

quickly past Diane and the others and out of the building.

"Max is wrong," Kevin said. "That woman isn't nice at all."

"Yeah," Donna said. "Old people always like Diane." Donna turned and looked through the window. As she watched Mrs. Wilson walk off, Donna said, "This may be another Fish Snitch mystery."

"What?" Kevin, Gary, and Diane asked.

"Mrs. Wilson reminds me of a movie I saw on television, *Tuna Fish Snitch.* A little girl was sick in bed. She sat by her window all day. Every morning she saw her neighbor go shopping. When she left the house, her neighbor was thin. When she came back, she was fat, with lumps and bumps all over."

"Why was she lumpy?" Diane asked.

Donna whispered, "That was the mystery. Then one day the girl saw a can of tuna fish and a bag of potato chips fall from her dress. The woman was stealing from the grocery."

"Why does that movie remind you of Mrs. Wilson?" Kevin asked.

"Mrs. Wilson is our neighbor just like that lumpy woman was the girl's neighbor. And I think the Wilsons are up to something. That's why they're acting so strange. I'm not even sure that boy is their nephew."

CHAPTER THREE

The next morning the twins went with Donna and Diane's brother Eric and his friend Cam Jansen to visit the City Museum. On the first floor the children saw old picture postcards and paintings of the city. Diane pointed to one of the postcards and said, "Did you see this? Brodie's Department store was once a tiny store called Brodie's Five and Dime."

Upstairs they saw old city newspapers.

The headline on one of the newspapers was *City Spy Ring Caught.* Donna showed it to Diane, Kevin, and Gary and said, "I bet those Wilsons are spies."

On the bus going home, Donna said, "I saw Mr. Wilson leave the building this morning."

"Did you see tuna fish cans fall out of his dress? Or maybe a bicycle. Maybe he stole a bicycle for Barry," Kevin said.

"You can joke if you want to," Donna said. "But I saw him leave the building at six-thirty in the morning, just after the newsboy. I'd like to know what he was doing out so early."

"Maybe he was going to work," Diane said.

Kevin shook his head. "Max said Mr. Wilson is retired. He has no work to go to."

The children got off the bus. Eric and Cam stopped at the bicycle shop. The twins walked to the park.

"I'd like to know what *you* were doing up so early," Kevin asked Donna. "On school days you're never ready on time."

"School days are different. If I get up late, I just miss school. If I got up late today, I'd miss vacation."

In the park some small children were on the swings and slides. A few older children were flying kites. Donna and Diane raced around the baseball field. Gary and Kevin sat on a bench next to an old man.

"Do you want to hear a joke?" Gary asked the old man.

The old man looked at Gary. Gary smiled. The old man picked up his newspaper and walked to another bench.

"Kevin, maybe you want to hear the joke. It's about a silly store owner. He went out for a few minutes and put up a sign, 'Closed. Out to lunch.' When he came back and saw the sign, he sat down to wait for himself."

Kevin got up.

"Not you, too," Gary said. "The joke couldn't be that bad. I read it in a book."

"It's not the joke. I just think we should be going home. It's almost time for lunch."

Kevin waved his arms at Donna and Diane. They saw him and ran to the bench. Then they all walked home.

"Look," Donna said as they got close to their apartment building. She pointed across the street to Mr. Wilson. He was carrying two large shopping bags.

"He's walking away from the building," Donna whispered. "I'll bet those bags are filled with evidence and he's getting rid of it."

"What kind of evidence?" Gary asked.

"Something terrible probably happened to Barry and now the Wilsons are getting rid of his clothing."

Diane shook her head and told her sister, "You're making all this up. You watch some dumb *Fish Snitch* movie and right away you think two nice old people are criminals."

"Those 'nice old people' wouldn't let us near their nephew. They sneak out of the building early in the morning. And now they're dumping two shopping bags filled with Barry's clothing."

"I'll bet you're wrong," Diane said.

"Maybe Mr. Wilson went shopping this morning. He was almost home when he remembered something he needed. Maybe it's something important, like vitamins or toothpaste. He went right back to get it."

"Let's go inside and wait," Kevin said. "If Mr. Wilson comes back carrying the shopping bags, we'll know Diane is right."

"And if he comes back without them, you'll know I'm right," Donna said.

CHAPTER FOUR

"Don't walk there," Max said to the twins as they came into the building. "I just washed the floor."

The twins walked along the side of the lobby, where it was dry. Kevin helped Max carry the mop and bucket into the laundry room. The others sat on one of the chairs in the lobby and waited for Mr. Wilson.

The front door opened. It was Mrs. Baxter.

"Be careful. The floor is wet," Diane told Mrs. Baxter.

"Where's Max?" she asked.

Max walked out of the laundry room. Mrs. Baxter held up a newspaper and said, "Do you see this? I had to go out and buy it. The newspaper boy didn't deliver my paper."

"That's odd," Max said. "My newspaper was in front of my door this morning."

"And I saw the delivery boy," Donna said.

"Well," Mrs. Baxter said as she walked into the elevator. "You tell that boy I expect my paper tomorrow."

Donna whispered to the others, "I'll bet Mr. Wilson had newspapers in those bags. He's stealing them."

The front door opened again and the twins turned to look. But it wasn't Mr. Wilson. It was the mailman. Diane and Gary helped him sort the mail while Donna and Kevin talked to Max.

Donna told Max about the movie *Tuna Fish Snitch*. Kevin told Max that the Wilsons were acting funny. Mrs. Wilson wouldn't talk to Diane. And they wouldn't let their nephew near anyone.

"Have you seen Barry since yesterday?" Donna asked Max.

"No."

"Maybe Barry went home," Kevin said.

"No. When he came, I helped the Wilsons carry the luggage. If Barry left, they would have asked me to help carry it down."

Donna jumped up. She pointed to the door and said, "Look at that. I'm right. The Wilsons *are* up to something."

Mr. Wilson was coming through the door. He was carrying the two shopping bags. But the bags were empty and folded.

Max held the door open and smiled. The old man didn't even look at Max. He walked quickly through the door, past Donna and Kevin and into the elevator.

"Diane, Gary, come here, quickly!" Donna called. When they came, Donna told them about the empty shopping bags. Then she said, "I'm going upstairs. I'll find out what's going on in the Wilson apartment."

"Don't bother those nice people," Max said.

Just then the elevator door opened. It was Mr. Russell. "Max," he said, "I have to talk to you about my TV. It's broken again."

The twins got into the elevator. "Remember what I told you," Max called as the elevator door closed.

When the door opened on the second floor, Donna said, "I'll knock on their door and say I must see Barry."

"You just can't do that," Diane said, as she pulled on her sister's sleeve. "Max told us to leave them alone."

"Let's just watch their apartment," Kevin said. "We can sit in the stairwell. If they do anything strange, we can tell Max or we can call the police."

The children walked quietly through the hall. When they passed 2B, the Wilsons' apartment, Donna stood close to the door and listened.

"I don't hear anything," Donna whispered.

The door to the stairs was across from 2B. The twins sat on the floor inside the stairwell. Donna kept the door open a crack with her foot.

The children waited. But nothing happened.

"I'm bored," Kevin said.

"I'll tell jokes," Gary whispered. "If I want to be a comedian, I have to practice."

Gary stood. He smiled and bowed. "Thank you. Thank you," he whispered. Then he bowed again and said, "You know, I haven't always been a comedian. I was a submarine captain until I opened a window. I was a magician until I made myself disappear."

"Sh," Donna said.

Gary whispered, "I was a frog. But I wasn't hoppy."

"Stop it," Donna said. "You're making me sick."

Kevin walked upstairs and made peanut butter sandwiches for everyone. The children ate while they watched the door of apartment 2B.

The door of 2E opened. A woman came out and went into the elevator.

"Do you know what's green and goes up and down?" Gary asked. "It's a pepper in an elevator."

After the twins finished eating, Diane gave each of them a napkin. She took her napkin and cleaned up the crumbs on the floor.

Then the door of 2B opened. Mrs. Wilson walked out. She was carrying two empty paper shopping bags. She pressed the button for the elevator and waited.

"Let's follow her," Kevin whispered.

"No," Donna said. "That's not what happened in *Tuna Fish Snitch*. The little girl in that movie never left her house. She just looked through her window."

"You and Diane stay here and watch the apartment," Kevin said. "Gary and I will follow Mrs. Wilson."

Kevin and Gary started down the steps just as Mrs. Wilson went into the elevator.

CHAPTER FIVE

"Sh. Wait here," Kevin whispered when they reached the lobby. "I don't want Mrs. Wilson to know we're following her."

He opened the door to the lobby and looked out. Kevin and Gary watched Mrs. Wilson leave the building.

They followed her to a grocery store. The boys went inside and pretended to be shopping. Gary pushed a shopping cart. Kevin put some ice cream, cat food, and sponges into the cart.

"There she is," Kevin whispered. "Let's walk past her and see what's in her cart."

As the boys walked toward Mrs. Wilson, Kevin asked Gary, "Now where do they have Sweet Sugar Kissed cereal? We have to find that cereal."

When they came to the next aisle, Gary said, "We don't need cereal."

"I didn't want her to know we were spying on her."

"Well," Gary said. "While you were looking for cereal, I looked into her cart. She had two large cartons of orange juice and two bottles of soda."

"Look, she's leaving the store," Kevin said. "And the ice cream is melting. We have to put this stuff back and get outside before we lose her."

The boys got outside just in time to see Mrs. Wilson walk into a drugstore down the

block. When they walked into the store they saw Mrs. Wilson take a pink and yellow container of No More Itch from one of the shelves.

Kevin and Gary hid behind a display of baby powder. When Mrs. Wilson left the store, they followed her. They saw Mrs. Wilson walk into the apartment building. The boys waited. When they thought she was already upstairs, they walked toward the building.

"Ugh!" they both said. The underground sprinkler had just turned on. Kevin and Gary were soaked.

Max ran outside. He saw the sprinklers spraying the sidewalk and the boys. "I better shut this off," Max said. And he ran into the building.

Water dripped from Kevin and Gary as they walked through the lobby. They quickly walked up the stairs to the second floor. Donna and Diane were sitting on the floor,

looking through the small opening in t
stairwell door.

"Look what happened to us," Gary said. He shook his head and water sprayed onto the floor.

"Sh," Donna told him. She pointed to two women talking in the hall.

"This is the third morning this week that I haven't gotten my newspaper," one woman said. She was carrying a bag of groceries and searching in her pockets for the key to her apartment door.

The other woman was holding a small dog. "Well," she said as she petted the dog, "I was up early to walk Fifi. It was about six o'clock. And the newspaper was right on my doorstep."

The women talked about the weather. The woman with the dog thought it would rain later in the day. But Donna was no longer listening.

Donna pulled her foot from the door and

let it close. Then she said, "Did you hear what they said about their newspapers?"

"Newspapers!" Kevin said in a loud voice. "We just followed Mrs. Wilson all over town."

"And we were soaked by some mixed-up sprinkler," Gary said. "And you want to talk to us about newspapers!"

Diane whispered, "That woman with the groceries isn't the only person who didn't get a paper. Mrs. Baxter told Max that she didn't get one. But Max and that woman holding Fifi got papers."

"And I saw the newspaper boy at six-thirty this morning," Donna said. "But that woman with the dog said she picked up her paper at six. Now maybe you can tell me how she can pick up her paper *before* the boy was even here!"

"Well, we still have another mystery to solve," Kevin said. Then he told Donna and Diane what Mrs. Wilson bought at the grocery and at the drug store.

"Did you see her steal any tuna fish cans or bags of potato chips?" Diane asked.

Gary shook his head and said, "We saw her pay for everything she took. She's not stealing things."

"If we want to find out what happened to Barry, we have to do what that little girl did in *Tuna Fish Snitch.* We have to watch the apartment," Donna said.

"It's silly for all of us to sit here," Kevin said. "Let's take turns. I'll change out of these wet clothes and get something to read. Then I'll watch the apartment for the first hour."

"I'll watch with you," Diane said.

"Me, too," Donna said.

"I guess I'll watch, too. It's no fun being in the apartment alone," Gary said.

Kevin and Gary changed into dry clothes. Kevin brought a book for each of the children to read. He brought a book about Harold Lloyd for Gary. He brought *The Underwater Fish Mystery* for Donna and *The Inside-Out Cat* for Diane. Kevin was reading a biography of Albert Einstein.

The twins sat in the stairwell all afternoon. People came and left their apartments. After five o'clock, people came home from work. But the door of apartment 2B didn't open.

The twins took turns eating supper. Then, at eight o'clock, Mrs. Shelton told Donna and Diane to come upstairs.

"I'll stay a little longer," Kevin told the girls.

"Me, too," Gary said. "I'm reading about Harold Lloyd's movies and they're very funny."

"I'll be back early tomorrow morning," Donna said, as she walked upstairs. "I want to see where Mr. Wilson goes so early."

"And what happens to those newspapers." Diane added.

CHAPTER SIX

Donna woke up early the next morning. She got out of bed quietly and went to brush her teeth. When she came back, Diane was sitting up in bed. But Donna didn't notice her.

Donna slowly opened her dresser. She took out her clothes and then walked quietly to the other side of the room. She walked into the closet, turned on the light, and closed the door. When she came out of the closet, she had on her slacks, shirt, and socks. Donna crawled under her desk to get her sneakers.

"Why are you being so quiet?" Diane asked.

Donna jumped. She banged her head on the bottom of the desk. "You scared me," she told her sister.

"If you're going downstairs, wait for me," Diane said as she threw off her blanket. "I'll be ready in just a minute."

Soon Donna and Diane were in the second floor stairwell. Donna opened the door and looked out. The door to apartment 2B was closed. There were newspapers on the floor in front of a few apartment doors.

"What time is it?" Donna asked.

Diane looked at her watch and said, "Ten minutes after six."

The girls waited. The door to apartment 2E opened. A dog on a leash came out followed by a woman. The woman picked up her newspaper. Then she and her dog went into the elevator.

Diane sat on the stairs while Donna watched the hallway. Diane stretched out her arms and yawned.

"Come here," Donna whispered.

The elevator doors had opened. An older boy stepped out. He was carrying a large pile of newspapers.

"That's the boy I saw yesterday," Donna told her sister.

"But the newspapers were already delivered," Diane said.

There were newspapers on the floor in front of three apartment doors. The two girls watched the boy take the newspapers and add them to his pile. Then the boy got back into the elevator.

"He's stealing those papers," Donna said. "Let's follow him."

"Look," Diane said, and pointed to

apartment 2B. The door was beginning to open.

As Donna and Diane were watching the hallway, someone said, "What are you looking at?"

The girls jumped. Kevin and Gary were standing behind them.

"I'm so glad you're here," Donna said. "We solved the mystery of the missing newspapers. Someone is stealing them. It's a tall boy with blond hair, a blue sweater, and sneakers. He just got into the elevator. Hurry and follow him."

The boys ran down the stairs.

Donna and Diane looked into the hall again. Mr. Wilson was locking his door. He walked toward the elevator. Then he stopped. He went back into his apartment. He came out a minute later wearing a raincoat.

"I'd like to find out what happened to Barry," Donna whispered.

When Mr. Wilson got into the elevator, Donna and Diane walked down the stairs. They watched Mr. Wilson leave the building. They followed him.

CHAPTER SEVEN

As Donna and Diane were leaving the building, Gary ran up to them. "We couldn't find him," he said. "Kevin and I ran all around the block and we didn't see a boy wearing a blue sweater. We didn't see anyone at all."

"He's not out here," Kevin said when he reached the others.

"Come with us," Donna said. "We're following Mr. Wilson."

The twins watched as Mr. Wilson walked to the corner. They waited until he crossed the street before they followed him. It was still early in the morning. Very few people were outside.

"Don't walk too fast," Kevin said. "We don't want Mr. Wilson to know we're following him."

Mr. Wilson walked through the park. The twins followed him. As they were passing the swings Diane said, "We're wasting our time. We didn't see Mr. Wilson do anything wrong. We should be following that boy who stole the newspapers."

As Mr. Wilson walked, he stopped a few times and took deep breaths. After Mr. Wilson left the park he walked toward the Hamilton Shopping Mall.

While the twins waited at a corner for the traffic light to change, Diane said, "After that boy left the second floor, he didn't go outside. That's why Kevin and Gary didn't

find him. He went to the other floors in the building to steal more newspapers."

The traffic light turned green. The twins crossed the street. Mr. Wilson was looking in the window of Brodie's Department Store. The children waited for Mr. Wilson to walk ahead. Then they ran to the store.

"Maybe there's some secret code in the window," Donna said. "Or maybe this is where he's meeting his crime boss."

"Or maybe," Diane said, "Mr. Wilson is just going for an early morning walk. And he looked in the window to see what's on sale."

Overcoats, underwear, running suits, bow ties, and umbrellas were in the window.

Donna said, "If we use the first letters of all those things on sale, I'll bet we can spell something, a secret code."

"O, u, r, s, b, t, u," Donna said. Then she said those letters again. "O, u, r, s, b, t, u."

"Sour tub," Kevin said. "The letters spell 'sour tub.' "

"Or 'bus tour,' Gary said.

The twins followed Mr. Wilson to Zim's bakery. The store was crowded with people on their way to the train station buying buttered rolls and coffee. Donna looked through the window and saw Mr. Wilson buy three rolls, a jelly donut, and a large slice of crumb cake.

While the others looked through the bakery window, Diane walked to a large toy store at the corner. She looked through the window at a display of ten-speed bicycles. Diane walked around the corner and looked at the display of baseball bats and gloves.

As Diane began to walk back to the bakery, she looked across the street. She saw people rushing to the train. Then she saw something else. She stopped. She stared. Then she ran back to the bakery.

CHAPTER EIGHT

"Come with me! Come with me right away," Diane told the others when she reached the bakery.

"Don't be silly," Donna said. "We're watching Mr. Wilson. He'll be leaving the bakery soon."

"I've found the boy with the blue sweater."

Donna, Kevin, and Gary followed Diane to the corner. She pointed to a boy across the street selling newspapers.

"He gets up real early," Diane whispered, "and steals newspapers. Then he sells them. The only people in our building who get their papers are the ones who get up before he comes."

"What do we do now?" Gary asked.

"We tell the police," Kevin said.

A police car was parked near the train station. Donna told the two officers in the car about the newspaper boy and she said,

"You can call Max, the doorman at our apartment house. He'll tell you that people were missing their newspapers."

A public telephone was nearby. One of the officers spoke to Max. Then he and his partner spoke to the boy and led him into the police car.

Before the police drove off, they asked Donna her name. "We may need you to sign some forms," he said. "You saw him take the papers."

"So did I," Diane told the police. And she gave them her name, too.

The twins watched the police car drive off. Then they walked home. When they reached their apartment building, Max was waiting for them. He held the front door open and took off his hat as the twins walked past.

Max followed the twins into the building. He lowered his voice and said, "We interrupt this program to bring you a news bulletin. The Fourth Floor Twins have solved the *Mystery of the Missing Newspapers.*" Then Max smiled and said in his regular voice, "I'm very proud of you."

"But we still haven't solved the *Fish Snitch Mystery.*" Donna said.

"The what?" Max asked.

"We still don't know what happened to the Wilsons' nephew."

"Oh, he's getting better," Max said. "But I don't think it's safe for you to see him yet."

"Safe?" What's not safe about him?" Donna asked.

"He has chicken pox. He's highly contagious."

Diane laughed and said, "That's why the Wilsons didn't want Barry to go near us."

Gary said, "And that's why Mrs. Wilson bought a jar of No More Itch. Those chicken pox blisters can be real itchy."

"Well, it doesn't explain what Mr. Wilson

had in those shopping bags. And it doesn't explain why he was sneaking out of the building so early," Donna said.

"Mr. Wilson always takes an early morning walk," Max said. "He likes the exercise. And he probably had empty soda cans and bottles in those bags. He collects them. The stores give you money back when you return them."

Kevin told Max, "We can visit Barry. We've all had chicken pox. And once you've had it, you don't get it again."

Max took the twins to apartment 2B. He rang the bell. Mrs. Wilson opened the door.

"One of you spoke to me the other day," she said, and I was too upset to answer. I'm sorry. You see, my nephew is visiting with us and he got sick. Taking care of a child is a big job and I was so worried."

"That's all right," Diane said.

"Can we see your nephew?" Kevin asked.

"We've all had chicken pox."

Mrs. Wilson led the twins inside the apartment. Barry was lying on a couch. His face and arms were covered with red blotches and pimples. On the table next to him was a large glass of orange juice.

"We live in the building and we're sorry you're not feeling well," Diane said. "Chicken pox is no fun. But after a while it gets better."

"You would have had a good time with us," Donna said. "We caught a newspaper thief."

Kevin told Barry that when they hadn't seen him, they were worried. And he told Barry and the Wilsons about the movie Donna had seen, *Tuna Fish Snitch*.

"I saw that movie," Mr. Wilson said. "I hope you didn't think we were thieves, like the woman in that movie."

The twins looked at each other. Then Donna told the Wilsons everything. When

she told them she had thought there was a secret code in the clothing store window, everyone laughed.

Then Gary said, "Some people call laughter the best medicine. I'm studying to be a comedian. Do you want me to tell you some jokes?"

"Sure," Barry and the Wilsons said.

"Do you know what's yellow and goes in circles?" Gary asked. "It's a dizzy banana."

Barry smiled.

"And do you know how elephants climb trees? They sit in a seed and wait for it to grow."

Barry laughed.

Kevin, Donna, and Diane looked at each other.

Then Gary said, "Do you know what's black, white, and red all over? It's a zebra with chicken pox."

Barry laughed again.

Donna put her hands on her cheeks and said, "I think I'm getting a fever. I'll need some of Barry's medicine. Gary's jokes are making me sick."